This Walker book belongs to:

_____

_____

_____

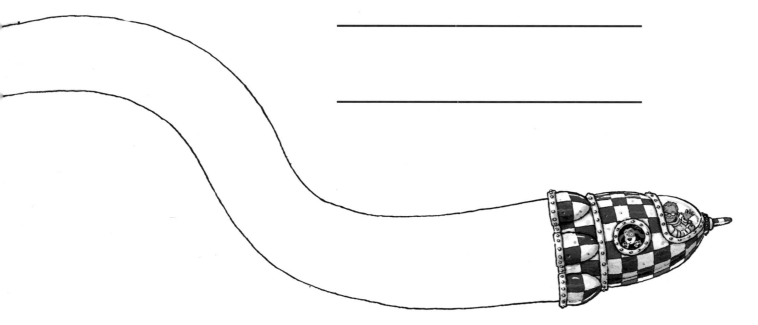

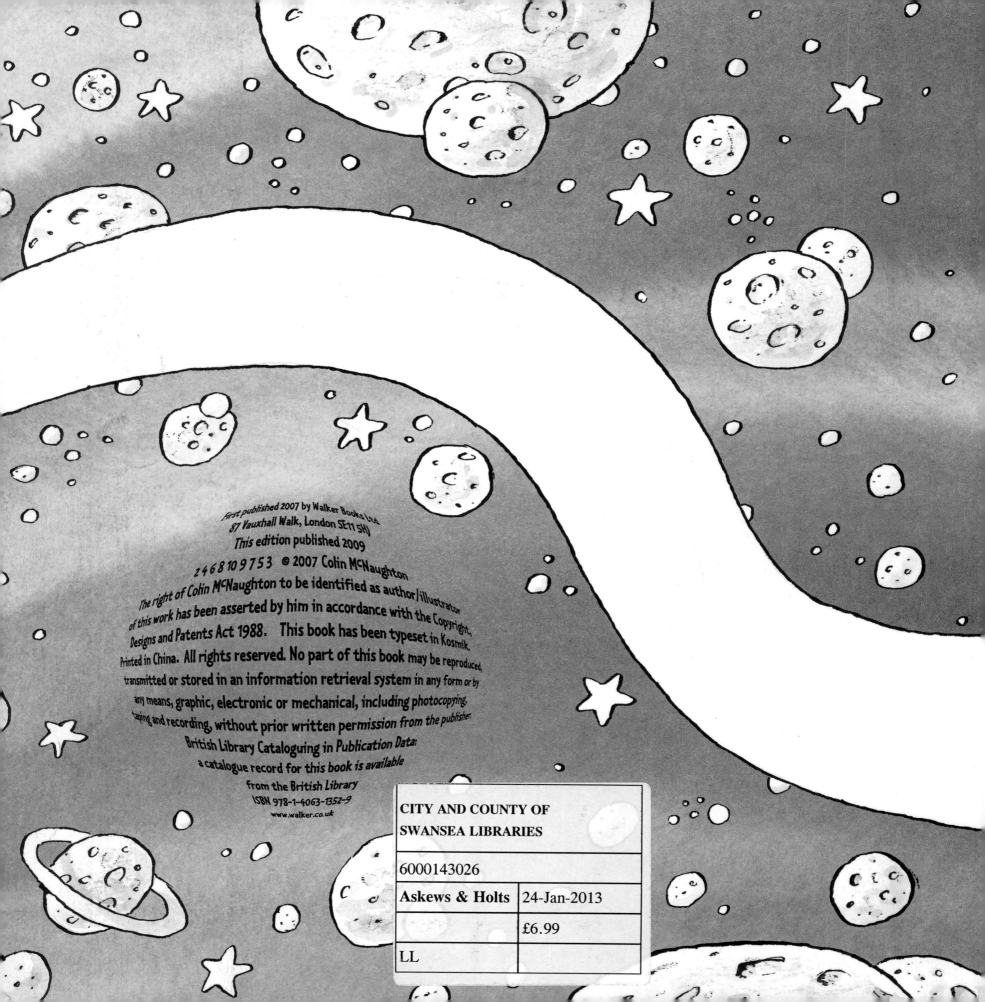

First published 2007 by Walker Books Ltd
87 Vauxhall Walk, London SE11 5HJ
This edition published 2009

2 4 6 8 10 9 7 5 3 © 2007 Colin McNaughton

British Library Cataloguing in Publication Data:
a catalogue record for this book is available
from the British Library
ISBN 978-1-4063-1352-9
www.walker.co.uk

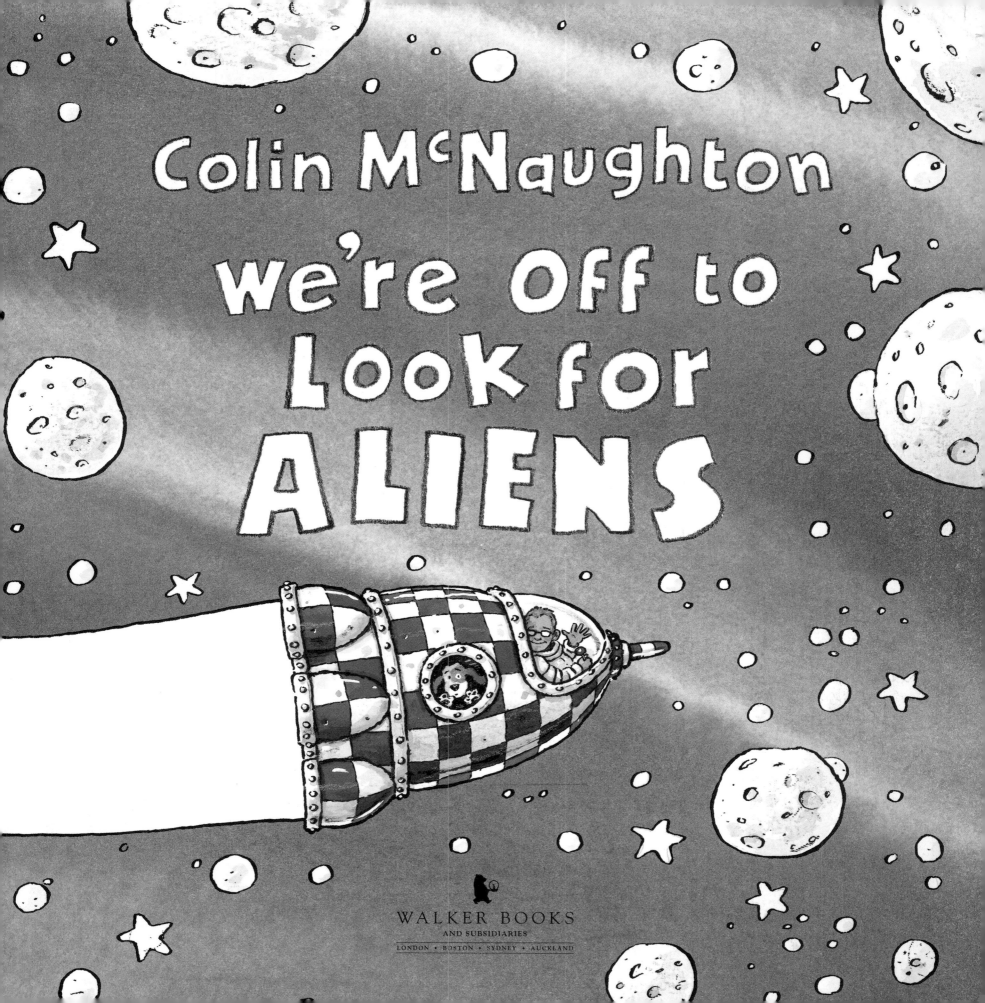

Colin McNaughton

We're off to
Look for
ALIENS

WALKER BOOKS
AND SUBSIDIARIES
LONDON · BOSTON · SYDNEY · AUCKLAND

"Ah-ha!" said Dad.
"My alien book. Thank you,
Mister Postman."

It was Dad's new book, fresh from the printer. Dad writes children's books. He also does the pictures. He says it's hard work – although he seems to spend an awful lot of time messing about.

"Tell me what you think,"
said Dad, handing us the book.
"I hope you like it."

"Tell me what you think,"
said Dad, handing us the book.
"I hope you like it ."

Dad said he was too nervous
to watch us read, so he took
the dog for a walk.

This is what we read

"Well," said Dad, back from his walk,
   "what do you think of my alien book?"
"It's brilliant, Dad," said my
   brother. "But there's a problem."
"What sort of problem?" frowned Dad.
"Well," said Mum carefully. "It's a
   great book and kids will love the pictures,

but ... it's the story."
"What's wrong with it?" said Dad.
"It's a wonderful story!"
"Yes, Dad," I said. "We agree.
It's just that children like
fairy tales and stuff, and
we were wondering, Dad ...

...who's going
to want to read
A *TRUE*
STORY?"

Other books by
Colin McNaughton

The Aliens are Coming!
ISBN 978-1-4063-1212-6

Here Come the Aliens
ISBN 978-0-7445-4394-0

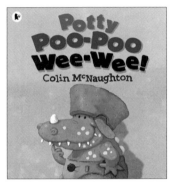

Potty Poo-Poo Wee-Wee
ISBN 978-1-4063-0131-1

Nighty Night
ISBN 978-1-4063-1241-6

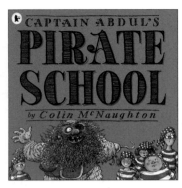

Captain Abdul's Pirate School
ISBN 978-0-7445-9896-4

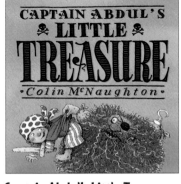

Captain Abdul's Little Treasure
ISBN 978-1-4063-0585-2
(PAPERBACK AND CD)

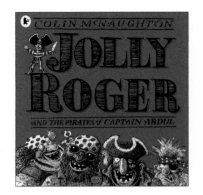

Jolly Roger
ISBN 978-1-84428-478-8

Available from all good bookstores

www.walker.co.uk